A collection of short stories of Shaam's Journey

Idea and Vision

Michelin Youssef

Writer

Samer Zarour

Paintings and Arts

Assaad Hanash

Contents

First short story... The Village -

Second short story... Shaam Story-

Third short story... TheRoad -

First Story
The Village

Everything Shaam loves and knows is in her little village, the trees and the school, her father, mother, cheerful brother, and her friend Jasmine.

Her father had a piece of land on the outskirts of the village which he inherited from his father. The land was full of fruit trees such as peach, plum, and apricot. "It is just like the little children as it needs care all the time," that is what he used to say when she asks him why he spends most of his time at the land.

Shaam used to tell her friends at school that her grandparents planted seeds in the land. They irrigated it till it overflowed, and then they slept beside the seeds every day till they became a long tree whose trunk split and her father got out of it, therefore; the color of his skin is similar to that of the land, his feet are firm like the roots, and his arms are long like the branches.

Her mother inherited nothing from her parents except many folkloric songs as she spent most of her time singing them to the extent that family members were able to know their mother's mood through what she is singing, and they sometimes knew what she wanted.

But the greatest event in Shaam's life was the birth of her little brother Ram as he used to have thick hair contrary to most newborns, in addition to his tiny features, naughty eyes, and little mouth which made her believe that her brother was in reality a squirrel and she became sure of that after he started to spend most of his time between the arms of her father as squirrels must be on the branches of the trees.

Shaam had a close friend called Jasmine, whose parents were the friends and neighbors of Shaam's parents for a long time, and Jasmine was of the same age as Shaam, and they went to school together and spent most of their time together.

Jasmine had an old doll that her grandmother made of cloth and stuffed with wool.

Jasmine and her doll remain together all the time even when she goes to school as she takes the doll with her, and puts it in her bag, and even when her parents bring new dolls for her, she used to throw them away and get back to her worn-out doll.

On a summer day, while the two friends were practicing their favorite ritual of lying on the grass and staring at the sky, Shaam asked Why you don't give your doll a name?

Jasmine stared at her and said as if she is telling her a secret "One day she will have a name, but not now."

SO when? Shaam asked. "When I live inside her," Jasmine said with full confidence.

Shaam laughed hard and held the doll and shook it in front of Jasmine's face, saying But you will not fit inside the doll, you are naive."

Jasmine clasped her hands under her head and said it is very simple, I will put the wool which is inside me inside her because I want to remain a little child."

Shaam answered "I can't wait to become a big girl to help my father at the farm and to help my mother in the kitchen and take care of my squirrel.

Jasmine whispered in Shaam's ear "If you come to us one day and don't find me ... Don't be afraid, I will be inside the doll. Take it with you, and then you can call her Jasmine and she will be your friend forever."

Shaam stared at the sky for a moment while thinking, then she asked Why you are looking at the sky?

She answered carelessly "I don't have a specific reason, but when you lie on your back, you don't have any place to look except the sky

Shaam continued "But I have a reason.'1 She kept silent for a while, and she continued

"I want the sky to know me and to remember my face and I want to build a new relationship with it because one day, I might ask her for a favor, and it is the source of rains and without rains, the trees will not grow and the people and animals will be thirsty.

Jasmine answered sarcastically" If the sky asks you who this girl lying beside you all the time I wish that you will say good things about me."

The two friends laughed hard and then Jasmine sat down, and she referred to the hill near them and said "Let's run to that hill and see what is there on the other side."

Shaam looked to where Jasmine pointed out and said "I will run with you anywhere if I keep seeing the water tank of our village. In my whole life, I haven't gone to any place where I didn't see the water tank."

Jasmine looked at her with astonishment "Not once!" Shaam answered, "Not once … everything I care about is here."

Jasmine adjusted her sitting position and said "You don't want to know anything about the world."

With the same quiet tone, she answered "We have a television at home, but we rarely watch it… I know that the world is big, but I decided to leave it for the rest of the people if they leave this place to me." Jasmine bent down and pulled Shaam from her hand and said "Come on lazy girl, you will see the water tank from the top and you will enhance your relations with the sky as the hill is closer to it … come on."

The two girls ran to the hill preceded by their laughs, but what they didn't know is that a storm was forming on the horizon, and it will destroy everything in their small world.

Shaam didn't fully understand what changed around her, yet her village is no longer as it used to be ... Something changed in the faces. Even her house is no longer the same. Only her little squirrel stayed the same as he is jumping in the house as if he owns the place.

Cars full of furniture are leaving the village and the neighbors are bidding farewell to each other as if they will not meet again.

Her father became more nervous, and he no longer allowed her to leave the house. Once, she got fed up and tried to object, but her father quickly replied using a term that he rarely uses "Obey me, girl". Shaam was not able to sleep that night and she remained awake in her bed searching for a happy idea that will make her sleep, but she failed, and tiredness overcame her as she closed her eyes, and as soon as her eyelids touched each other, the world around her went crazy. All the scary sounds that they were hearing from afar became between the streets and the houses of the village. She felt that the ground is shaking under her. The sun hadn't shined yet, but the light was intense outside her window.

The fire was everywhere.

Her father got out of his room shouting "Get away from the window", and he pulled her from her hand in a painful way.

The village was still burning outside, but inside the two children collected all their possessions of money in the house and everybody got out of it. Nobody bid farewell to what his eyes used to see every day throughout the years. Only her father, while closing the door addressed his house saying "Please stay as you are ... We will come back soon," and he put the key with the money inside a small purse that he put on his waist.

The streets of the village were like the resurrection day. All the locals were running in the same direction as if a flood is chasing them.

After they reached the outskirts of the village, the father suddenly stopped and said to his wife "Take the children away ... I will look for our neighbors. I didn't see them among the people." Shaam ran behind her father because she wanted to see her friend Jasmine. Her mother called her many times, but she didn't pay attention. on. She saw her father at a place that used to be of their neighbors, and they saw a very ugly scene as there were just piles of stones covering other piles. Her father stood on the ground and hit his head with his hands, shocked by the loss. He realized that it might be the first farewell of a series that he fears that will be long. Shaam got close to the pile of stones and she lifted some stones in her little hands "They might be hiding in some corner." She looked at her father as if she is asking for companionship for her desperate idea, but who did that to their neighbor's house was careful not to keep any corner to hide in.

Her father grabbed her from her hand while trying to overcome his sadness "We can't do anything. " his voice was stronger than all the noise around them.

"Jasmine" Shaam called her with a voice choked with tears "I promised her."

Her father wasn't in a better condition, but he doesn't enjoy the luxury of honesty:

don't be sad .... they might have left before us."

Shaam chose to believe her father because this was much easier than the grief, and while she was about to leave, a faint voice called her "Shaam". She looked for the source of the voice and there on the ground, she saw eyes staring at her. It was the old doll.

Shaam lifted it from the ground, and the doll whispered in her ear "I was sure that you will come."

"I will not leave my best friend," Shaam said while she was wiping her tears away with great enthusiasm, "I have a name now," the doll said ... Shaam embraced her and said "Jasmine ... we will remain with each other forever as we had agreed." Jasmine sighed "It is better because
I hate loneliness."

After they became outside their village and while walking away, Shaam raised her face from
her father's shoulder, and she looked at the village "Look Jasmine ... the water tank is still there."

"As if the village also is bidding farewell to us," she said sadly.

The two friends kept watching the water tank till it was out of their sight.

- End of the First Story-

Second Story
Shaam Story

Shaam walked away from the noisy group of children. She was not sad or bored from playing but she wanted to know the place more, there is a lot of trees here, maybe it looks like her home but it's not. She saw a wooden chair and decided to stand upon it so she can have a bitter view.

She stood on the chair and then on her toes. She did not see a lot but she smiled as she saw a green mountain far away on the horizon. Green was her favorite color.

She was tired so she sat down.

"How are you, little child?" Shaam heard a voice calling her so she turned toward the voice.

He was a new person that she didn't meet before. He had this big round face, kind eyes, and a wide smile drawn on his face.

Shaam said to herself while she looked to the ground: "Why does his face look so familiar."

She scratched her nose a little bit and then she figure it out: "Aha ..... Now I know why,

The looks exactly like the snowman we used to make in our village during winter. She laughed trickily, I will call him "The Snow Man ".

She smiled and looked at him: "I am good. Thank you for asking "

"Why are you alone? "The snowman asked.

"I am not alone but I prefer to set here for now."

"Where are your parents" In confidence she replies 'they will be here soon... I know that for sure"

"Why don't you play with the other kids .... did they annoy you? "

She pointed to a kid in the group "That is my brother who is playing there and he doesn't let anyone annoy me"

"Are you hungry? "Shaam begins to feel bored "No at all. ... I am just dreaming"

The snowman moved his big head "Dreaming!!!. ... But you need to sleep so you can dream "

"No" Answered Shaam "I dream whenever I want to .... All I have to do is to close my eyes for
a while,"

"Okay then .... close your eyes and tell me what you see ".

Shaam closed her eyes for a moment and then she smiled and laid her head on the wall. ...

The snowman whispered: "Didn't we agree that you tell me what you see? "

She gave him a look of reproach and said: "Don't be hot-headed, let me enjoy it a little bit, oh ... how I miss my home "

The snowman stood silently with his arms pinned together and without noticing he started clicking on the ground restlessly.

"Stop please" Said Shaam "You are very big and I am a little child and my dreams are small and fragile so if you keep clicking on the ground with your giant feet all my dreams may collapse forever ".

The snowman stopped moving and he looked at his feet "Wow, they are really gigantic "

He stared at her like a little puppy "I am sorry ….. I hope that I didn't do much damage ".

"You nearly destroyed our neighbor's house …. Her name is Om Foa'd … you know something….. She has two noisy cows, they always mooing at each other all day long… It is just like they are having this never-ending conversation ".

"Om Foa'd probably hate those two noisy cows ".

"No …. Actually it is totally the opposite … she takes care of them like they were her own children and they give her in return a very delicious milk, and she uses it to make yogurt, cheese, butter, and margarine ".

"I like butter "He said that and he started feeling his stomach. "Tell me more, what do you see?". "I see everything in my village, every house, every street, and even the trees leaves and the cicada sleeping there.

"And what do you miss the most ".

What an amazing feeling, it is just like there is an electric wire that transfers happiness and joy from one heart to another ".

Shaam stood on the chair and she raised her hands high and then she bow down just like the actors do at the end of the show and she screamed: "I will be a theatrical ".

The snowman looked at her and said: "That is great, maybe I will do that also " "But you cannot" and she put her hands on her waist.

The snowman looked at her and said: "That is great, maybe I will do that also " "But you cannot" and she put her hands on her waist.

"Why "?

"You need to have magical powers to be a theatrical ".

Shaam jumped from the wooden chair down to the ground "Don't you see how they change their dresses and the way they look within just a few seconds, and how they change their voices and movements without you even notice .... How they make you happy or sad .... how they make you laugh and cry at the same moment. .... You have to be a magician to do such a thing ".

The snowman stood up and walked beside her "And how are you planning to use these magical powers? "

She took a deep sigh "Oh .... I need to work hard because there is a lot of suffering and pain where I came from ".

"Come closer, "she said to him.

The snowman got down on his knees and with one jump Shaam climbed over his shoulders. The snowman stood up and started walking around the place. The other kids saw them and gathered around them happily.

"You see ... When you stand on the stage you can see all the people, and that is what I am going to do.

If I saw someone falling down off his bicycle, I will be a doctor so I can treat his wounds and get him back on the bicycle again. And when I see a burning house I will quickly become a fireman with a long hose to put the fire down and save everybody in the house.

But if I saw a child who cry out of hunger " she snapped her fingers " with just one move
I will become a hard-working farmer and I will plant all the fields with vegetables and fruits so no child will ever be hungry on this earth again.

At this moment the kids started to shout her name "Shaam Shaam Shaam"

The snowman put her down on the ground "I will be honored to see one of your shows."

With a gentle move, Shaam raised her dress's edges and archly bowed her knees down "I will try to save a place for you in the first row because we are friends now .... Aren't we? "

"Of course, we are friends "

The snowman left Shaam with the other kids and walked away ..... Shaam followed him with her eyes and said quietly "What a nice snowman, I hope that he does not melt down in the summer ".

She laughed and then run along with the other kids, looking for a new game ....

The End of The Second Story -

Third Story
The Road

The inhabitants of the village continued to walk carrying their memories on their backs, and walking in a huge space without any features.

Shaam wanted to know when this march will continue, so she asked her father who used a
the word she has never heard before "till reaching the borders"
That is what he said.

Yet Shaam didn't understand the meaning of the word because she has never crossed the
borders in her life, and when her father saw bewilderment in her eyes, he said to her "You want me to explain to you."

Shaam nodded with acceptance, and her father continued "It is something invented by humans since ancient times to stay away from each other. "

"Why?" she asked with great enthusiasm.

"Some of them have different grandfathers and different skin colors. Some of them look at the sky in a different way and some of them don't want people to see what they are doing."

"I didn't like that idea of the borders. Is not it better if people meet with each other?"

He smiled at the innocence of his daughter "Some people prefer to remain alone."

"Oh, it is regrettable, How do these borders look like?"

"you will know them when we reach them."

Shaam looked at Jasmine who seemed to have something to say "Say what you want," Shaam encouraged her.

"We the dolls don't have borders between us and we meet in any wardrobe or drawer without any dispute or differentiation ."

"How nice are you? I wish I can join you."

"You can't do that," Jasmine said "You don't have enough wool inside you."

Her father was right as Shaam knew borders when she saw them. She saw barbed wire and high towers with angry men on their top and around them.

They allowed them to enter beyond the borders like the others. They gave them a big smile and told them that they will stay temporarily till returning home. They allowed them to enter and closed the doors, and they forgot them or ignored them.

All the cold days and hot days passed away, and the sun rose from their east and went down from their west three hundred and sixty-five times.

Yes, a year passed away and now there is no trace of the big smiles, and what was temporary now seems to be eternal.

Houses in this place look like matchboxes or Lego pieces, all of them are the same and they have the same distances between them. Children laughing and playing were drawn on their walls, yet there is no happy child in this place as if happiness can be hung up on the wall.

A few days later, the father gathered them in their matchbox and he said, "I want you to get ready ... we will go to the sea." Shaam and Ram looked at each other with enthusiasm because any place will be better than where they are, but their mother didn't want that, yet the father was determined "Pack your luggage... we will leave in the morning."

"What an exciting idea," Shaam told Jasmine.

Jasmine answered with the same enthusiasm "Have you seen the sea before?"

Shaam shook her head saying "No, but I know that it is very small as it used to fit into our TV."

Before sunrise, the family packed their little belongings and they slipped towards the gate "We will go on the train towards the sea," the father said that this was the plan.

When they arrived, Shaam approached the shore while she was amazed at the greatness
and solemnity of the sea. Its roaring sound and limitless range. Jasmine said while she was between Shaam's arms "How many TVs do you need to contain all of this?"

Shaam didn't pay attention to Jasmine's comments as she was fully captivated. She got nearer and wanted to touch the water to believe, and as soon as her fingertip touched the cold water, she felt a great awe and fear "How are we going to pass across it? ... How will we be allowed to ride it? ....."

Jasmine told her "Why don't you try to talk to it as you used to do with the sky in the village?"

Shaam liked the idea "I will try ... " She closed her eyes for a moment trying to organize her ideas and to choose her words carefully as the sea has inescapable solemnity when you stand on the sand of its shore.

"O great sea ... Please allow me and my family to pass."

Jasmine interrupted her "Me too... tell it about me."

Shaam looked at her repentantly "Don't interrupt me ... We don't want to make it angry."

Jasmine said very shyly "I don't want it to swallow me ... I wish that it doesn't like the cloth and wool. .. and I don't think that I will make a difference for it. .. look at its seize."

Shaam put her hand at Jasmine's mouth and said "Hshhh ... I will tell it about you."

She took a deep breath and continued "O great sea ... I wish that you will allow me and my family and my friend Jasmine to pass into where life is better ... We are forced to do that because our village had been taken by angry men ... They took my trees, books, school and a little tree which my mother planted in the garden, and they even stole words from the mouth of my little brother and nothing was left for us ... If you want to make sure, you can ask the sky as I have told her everything ... I think that you are relatives because you are very similar to each other."

All of them got on board a little boat inside which people crowded and there was no place for any breath of air.

As soon as the boat started to move, Shaam's heart was beating so fast as she has never experienced such a feeling before.

There was a little child who was about the same age as Shaam. He squatted down in front of her catching the arm of his mother. She stared at him for a while and said "We will arrive, the sea promised me."

The boy smiled and said, "If the boat capsizes, I will hold your hand so you will not drown." She was overwhelmed with a unique feeling of peace even though she was at sea, not only due to what the nice boy said, but the situation of sitting beside each other was not only due to the small size of the boat but because they were in the same journey, they will either arrive or sleep forever inside the abdomen of that huge blue monster.

There is no place similar to the sea which if it roars, it can smash the bravest men.

A wave behind another relentlessly hit the little collapsing boat which is filled with dreams.

The earth was not visible from any direction as they were at the mercy of the one who can't be trusted. Some people said "Let's return," but the owner of the boat cried out "It is impossible to return."

Somebody suddenly shouted "I see the land …. "It was an unbelievable scene at a short distance from them, yet their troubles haven't finished yet because the boat was moaning under the influence of the waves and the huge weight it carries aboard, and the water started to leak into the boat. The owner of the boat told them to empty it of water in any way or they will drown, and he told them not to try to jump or swim to reach the shore as the water is very cold and whoever falls in it will freeze before reaching the shore.

The young and elderly people started to empty the water out of the boat, but they didn't have anything except their palms to carry the water and put it back into the sea. They will not accept the def eat after they became very near to that extent.

There is no place similar to the sea which if it roars, it can smash the bravest men.

A wave behind another relentlessly hit the little collapsing boat which is filled with dreams.

The earth was not visible from any direction as they were at the mercy of the one who can't be trusted. Some people said "Let's return," but the owner of the boat cried out "It is impossible to return."

Somebody suddenly shouted "I see the land …. "It was an unbelievable scene at a short distance from them, yet their troubles haven't finished yet because the boat was moaning under the influence of the waves and the huge weight it carries aboard, and the water started to leak into the boat. The owner of the boat told them to empty it of water in any way or they will drown, and he told them not to try to jump or swim to reach the shore as the water is very cold and whoever falls in it will freeze before reaching the shore.

The young and elderly people started to empty the water out of the boat, but they didn't have anything except their palms to carry the water and put it back into the sea. They will not accept the defeat after they became very near to that extent.

Amidst the frenzy, a huge scream covered the sound of the waves "Talal," She was the mother of the child who promised Shaam to save her. He fell into the sea. His head was over the water, but the boat started to get away from him, "save him please," his mother shouted while crying, and people were trying to summon up all their courage to jump into the raging sea. They heard the sound of a body hitting the water, and they saw a man swimming toward Talal. Shaam was able to distinguish him through his long body and his twig-like arms. He was her father. He held Talal from his neck and swam back to the boat. When people pulled them out of the water, they were trembling and their skin was almost white and their lips were blue.

Shaam embraced her father while trying to warm him up, but he gently lifted her "Don't be afraid ... I am okay." Talal's mother came towards them her eyes were full of tears "Thank you, I owe you my life ... I lost his father, and I have no one except him in this life. "The father tried to answer, but his trembling lips prevented him from that, and Shaam answered II No need for thanks lady because my father says when you help someone in trouble, someone will help you when you need that."

When the boat touched the sand, it seemed as if it is a new birth to whoever was on board the boat as the sea allowed them to pass into the promised land where life is better than what they have imagined

The End of The Third Story -